13th STREET

Tussle with the Tooting Tarantulas

Read more 13th Street books!

HARPER**Chapters**

13thSTREET

Tussle with the Tooting Tarantulas

by **DAVID BOWLES**

illustrated by **SHANE CLESTER**

HARPER
An Imprint of HarperCollins*Publishers*

To my cat Kimi, for taking care of
all those spiders for me.

13th Street #5: Tussle with the Tooting Tarantulas
Copyright © 2021 by HarperCollins Publishers
All rights reserved. Printed in the United States of America.
No part of this book may be used or reproduced in any manner whatsoever
without written permission except in the case of brief quotations embodied
in critical articles and reviews. For information address HarperCollins
Children's Books, a division of HarperCollins Publishers, 195 Broadway,
New York, NY 10007.
www.harperchapters.com
Library of Congress Control Number: 2020949243
ISBN 978-0-06-300959-2 — ISBN 978-0-06-300958-5 (pbk.)
Typography by Torberg Davern and Catherine Lee
21 22 23 24 25   PC/LSCC   10 9 8 7 6 5 4 3 2 1

First Edition

CONTENTS

CHAPTER

1

THE ROAR AT THE RANCH!

The old house glowed bright and warm against the growing dark of a late winter afternoon. From every room came laughter and excited chatter. Dante Dávila felt happier than he had in a long time. His whole family was celebrating his great-grandfather Arturo's ninetieth birthday at Rancho el Monte— their ranch in Las Tunas, Mexico.

With the party about to begin in the living room, Dante could almost forget that in an hour or two he would return to the frightening, monster-filled world of 13th Street.

His grandmother had been staring at Dante for nearly a full minute. It wasn't just annoying. It was downright dangerous! All his life, adults had told him that if someone stared at him too long, he could get *mal de ojo*.

The evil eye!

Luckily, his grandmother reached out a wrinkled hand and rubbed his hair.

"Abuela Beba!" Dante groaned, though he was secretly relieved. "You're messing up my 'do!"

"Ay, Dante," said his mother, Lola. "You're cute even with your hair messed up."

"Don't worry, *m'ijo*," said his grandmother, "I wouldn't want you to get mal de ojo."

"No such thing as the evil eye," interrupted his mother. She set a paper plate in Dante's hands. It was piled high with tamales. "But you're looking kind of thin, m'ijo. Eat."

The food smelled delicious. As Dante unwrapped a *tamal*, he tried not to picture this as his last meal. "Did you know the Maya invented tamales? They needed some food they could carry with them on long trips. I read it in this book that—"

"Oh Dante," said his grandmother. "You don't need to study so hard. You're so handsome! Your looks will open doors for you."

Aunt Lucy shook her head. "No, Mom. Dante's more than just a pretty face."

Dante felt his cheeks get red. He set down his plate and stood. "Be right back."

He stomped off toward the patio door, but his mother followed him outside.

"Dante, are you okay?" she asked.

He sighed. "Mom, y'all are so annoying."

"Don't be angry. We're only complimenting you, m'ijo," she said.

She had a point. And Dante used to love all the attention. Now there were more important things on his mind. Two of his classmates had been pulled into a nightmare world of monsters and ghosts. Only Dante and his cousins could save them.

"I know. Sorry, Mom."

"Are you coming back in?" she asked.

"Bathroom run," he said, nodding toward the outhouse a few steps away.

"Hurry back," his mother said. "We're going to cut the cake soon. Then it's piñata time!"

Dante gave her a thumbs-up and ran outside. His cousins, Malia and Ivan, were waiting for him beside the outhouse.

"You're late," Ivan said.

"I got mobbed, dude," Dante explained.

"Is that Dante?" a voice said from Malia's phone. It was Susana on video chat.

Malia nodded at the screen. "Yes. He just escaped his fans."

"Um, whatever," Susana said, rolling her eyes. "Anywho, there's still no sign of Santiago and Rafaela, y'all. Mickey and I have been Skyping for the past few days. Because  of the portal that popped up on his map in the aquarium and then faded, we're totally convinced the two ended up on 13th Street."

Dante sighed. "Gah. I really wish Mickey was leading this rescue attempt. He knows 13th Street a lot better."

"Well, he's stuck in Japan with his parents," Susana pointed out.

"I know," Dante said. "Heck, even having you along would be a relief."

Susana raised an eyebrow. "Uh, thanks? I guess? But I don't have a passport, so I couldn't go to Mexico."

Ivan poked his head over his cousins. "Anyway. One of the portals is near the ranch, right?"

Without warning, the bathroom door opened:

WHAM!

The cousins jumped.

A horrifying growl came from inside the bathroom.

ROOOOOAAAARRRRR!

Malia pushed her cousins back, lifting her hand. "Close up, Ka—"

Ivan clamped his hand over her mouth. "Wait!"

Out of the bathroom came lurching . . .

. . . **DOÑA CHABELA!**

"*¡Ay, Dios mío!*" she laughed. "You kids nearly pooped your pants, huh?"

Dante clutched his chest. His heart was beating like a marching drum. "*¡No manche*, señora! That was **NOT FUNNY**!"

CHAPTER

2

SPOOKY SHACK

"Sorry!" Chabela giggled. "I couldn't resist."

Malia narrowed her eyes. "Oh, sure. Now that your grandson's safe, you're all fun and games."

Ivan cleared his throat. "Why are you even here? Susana's about to review the plan with us. We're all set."

"*Ay, chamaco*," Chabela said. "Mickey sent me. I'm, uh, logistical support or something.

I'll keep your parents off your trail."

"Let's hurry, then," Susana chimed in. "Mrs. Aguilar walks you to the portal and stands guard. Y'all reenter 13th Street and get the pikos to take you back through the sewers till you reach the zombie family. Then all of y'all head to the Depot of the Dead to negotiate with Omi for supplies."

Chabela nodded. "According to Mickey, the zombies and skeleton people know all the

movements of the woman with white hair I saw in my dreams. He calls her the Queen of Bones."

Dante gasped. "Queen of Bones?"

"*Sí*," Chabela said. "Mickey didn't explain much. He just said you should watch out for her. She's very dangerous."

"But she's probably got Santiago and Rafaela," Susana added. "Which is why you need to figure out where she is."

Malia groaned. "My phone's about to die, Susana. Quick question: What does she want with them? Did Mickey have any ideas?"

"Not really." Susana shrugged and adjusted her headset. "Just that the queen is obsessed with human kids. Something about our imaginations."

"Maybe that's why she appeared to you, Chabela," Ivan mused, "and asked you to send her children."

Somewhere, a door creaked open. An adult started shouting.

"Hey, *huercos*! Where are y'all? The party is about to start!"

With a shushing gesture, Chabela pulled the three cousins away. "Come! No time to lose!"

The sun had dropped below the horizon, leaving just a reddish glow in the sky. But the moon was out and nearly full. It was easy to follow the path to the big mesquite tree beside the well.

When they reached the mesquite, the cousins grabbed three backpacks they had hidden there. They'd filled them with stuff they might need: flashlights, rope, water guns full of mouthwash, earplugs, small fire extinguishers, and salt.

"We should leave our sweaters here," Ivan said. "Remember how hard it was to run in our snowsuits?"

Dante gave a little laugh as he carefully pulled his sweater over his head. "Guess we're serious monster hunters now, huh?" He patted his hair back into place.

Chabela snapped her fingers. "That reminds me. Mickey sent you a gift."

She rooted around in her purse and pulled out a squeaky toy.

"Um," Dante said, "how is that supposed to help?"

"It belonged to Bruno," Chabela explained. "If he hears this, that big dog will come running and defend you."

Dante stuck it in the front pocket of his backpack.

Chabela led them along the narrowing path through the brush. Soon they reached a spooky old shack.

"The portal is inside," she said.

"Cowboys used to live here," Ivan whispered, "a hundred years ago."

"Vaqueros, you mean," Malia corrected.

Dante shivered. "And now?"

"Just ghosts," Chabela said.

Dante breathed in relief. Ghosts weren't so bad.

"And maybe tarantulas," she added.

That made Dante stop dead in his tracks.

CHAPTER

3

A GRUMPY GHOST

Chabela nudged Dante. "You'll be fine. They don't bite. I'd be more worried about the Queen of Bones."

Dante shuddered. "*¡Uy, cucuy!*"

"Stop freaking Dante out, Doña Chabela. Time to move," Malia said, raising her hand. "Open, Hebaan!"

Though it had been nailed shut and was partly rotted, the door swung wide.

Something kind of big—a rat or opossum—skittered away from the moonlight that poured into the shack. There were cobwebs and leaves everywhere. Stepping carefully, Malia walked in, waving at her cousins to follow.

Dante grimaced but gave Chabela a thumbs-up. "See you when the mission is accomplished!"

The floor groaned under their feet.

CREEEAAAK!

Somewhere outside, a barn owl screeched like a frightened child.

SHRIIIIEEEK!

"See the portal yet?" Dante asked, trying to keep cobwebs out of his hair.

"There!" said Ivan.

Beside an old iron stove, the purple outline of a portal pulsed faintly.

"Okay, Chabela!" Malia called. "We're going through!"

She stepped into the purple glow and shimmered for a second. Then, **WHOOSH**! She disappeared.

Dante entered next. Passing through a portal was like walking through water. The humming grew loud in his ears, then **PLOP**!

He stepped into the nightmare world of 13th Street.

"Wait." Dante looked around as Ivan came through behind him. "This isn't a sewer, guys."

They were standing in a dusty living room. The furniture was covered with sheets.

"WHAT ARE YOU DOING IN MY HOUSE?!" an unfamiliar voice said.

The cousins spun around, gasping in surprise. Floating in the air nearby was a man. Well, the ghost of a man. He looked a lot like their

friend Yoliya. But bigger and uglier.

"This wasn't in the plan," Malia said.

Dante frowned. "What should we do now?"

"Excuse me, sir," Ivan said. "I'm looking for a couple of human kids."

"THERE ARE TWO STANDING RIGHT BESIDE YOU!" the grumpy ghost shouted.

Malia shook her head. "Not us. Other kids."

The ghost just glared at them.

"What about . . . the Queen of Bones?" Ivan asked.

The ghost floated back as if in fear. **"HUSH! DON'T MENTION HER NAME! JUST GET OUT!"**

Dante raised an eyebrow. "Okay, **BOO**-mer. Don't get your ectoplasm in a bunch."

Malia was already at the front door. "Open, Hebaan!"

They stepped outside, and the door slammed shut. Dante looked up and down the block. Broken-down houses, leaning at weird angles. Dead trees. Rusted cars.

None of it was familiar.

"Where the heck are we?" he asked.

CHAPTER

4

TERRIFYING TARANTULAS!

Malia balled her hands into fists. "It looks kind of like the first place we visited. But houses, not apartment buildings. Ivan?"

Ivan was a little distracted. He pointed at Dante's head. "Don't freak out, but . . . you've got some spiderwebs in your hair."

"What?" Dante hurried to the next house to check his reflection in a broken window.

Wispy webs were clinging to his wax-sculpted hairdo! With shaking hands, he carefully started picking the white strands from his hair.

Please, no spiders, he prayed silently.

"Are you afraid, or just super vain?" Malia asked.

Dante took a moment to really look at himself. He was here on an important mission. The stakes were high. But he couldn't stop picking at his hair.

"Oh!" Ivan exclaimed, kneeling beside a manhole cover. "We must be right above the sewer where Bruno and Mickey reunited."

Before Dante and Malia could respond, a strange sound filled the air.

SKITTER-SKATTER!
PITTER-PATTER!

And then over the rooftops they came.
HUGE, WOLF-SIZE TARANTULAS!

Dante's heart almost stopped.

The massive spiders crawled down crooked walls and leaped into trees. They were all headed in the same direction.

Straight toward the cousins!

Wow, you're really flying through these pages!

CHAPTER

5

FARTING AND FLYING?

"Run!" Malia screamed.

But Dante was already sprinting away. Spiders grossed him out, even little ones.

Tarantulas the size of wolves? Yeah, forget that.

Ivan and Malia caught up pretty quickly. From behind them came a loud trumpeting sound.

TOOOOOOOT!

The cousins slowed and looked over their shoulders. Their worry turned to amazement and shock.

The spiders were flying through the air!

TOOOOOOOT!

Another spider blasted off a rooftop, leaving a wake of shingles behind it.

"Are they . . . farting?" panted Malia.

"Oh, snap," Dante said. "You're right!"

One of the tarantulas landed about fifty yards away. It scrunched up its weird face and tooted again, rocketing into the air. A whirlwind of dust and gravel went spinning behind it.

"Methane propulsion," Ivan said in awe.

"Huh?" Malia asked. "Remember, I don't speak nerd."

"Fart power," said Dante, laughing. "And it's bringing them closer, fast."

"Hurry!" Malia ordered. "Find a door with the thirteen symbol on it! We need to get inside, now!"

CHAPTER

6

CASA DE CALACAS

The tarantulas kept tooting, flying closer and closer. The cousins rushed from house to house, checking the doors.

Finally they found one with the double bar and three dots. Number thirteen. Dante lifted his hand. "Open, Hebaan!"

BOOM! The door almost flew off its hinges. Inside, there was a family of skeletons—*calacas*, like Omi from the Depot of the Dead.

From their size and traditional Mexican clothing, it seemed like a mom, dad, and two children.

"*Papá*, who are they?" one of the kid calacas asked.

"No idea," he answered.

THUD! THUD! THUD!

A trio of terrifying tarantulas landed in the front yard.

"Get inside!" the mother calaca cried. "And lock the door!"

CHAPTER

7

SPIDER SIEGE!

The cousins didn't need the invitation—they were already rushing inside. Dante shut and locked the door behind them.

"Why did you let them in, Blanca?" the father calaca demanded.

His wife gestured at them. "They pretty much invited themselves, Cano."

WHAM!

Something heavy collided with the door. Everyone jumped.

The youngest calaca, a boy, started sniffling. "I'm scared!"

"Don't worry, Cándido," his father said, hugging him. "The Queen of Bones just wants these living children."

Dante gulped. "You're not going to give us up, are you?"

The skeleton girl spoke up. "Well, she's our ruler. It's hard not to obey."

WHAM!

The spiders weren't letting up.

"I thought Mickey Aguilar ruled 13th Street," said Ivan.

The calaca shook her head. Her bones made a sound like a marimba. "No. He's the Quiet Prince, but she's the Loud Queen. The one who rules. The tarantulas are her soldiers."

WHAM!

This time, a crack appeared in the door.

Dante glanced at the windows on either side of it. They were boarded up, but—

BASH! BASH! BASH!

One of the tarantulas started hammering away at the boards.

CREEEAAAK! The nails began to pull away from the window frame.

Malia pointed at the girl calaca. "What's your name?"

"Alba," she replied.

"Okay, Alba," Malia said. "Is there any place to hide? Because those tooting tarantulas are getting in whether we like it or not."

"Um, the attic?" Alba glanced over her shoulder. "There's also the garage."

Ivan snapped his fingers. "Does the garage door open?"

Cano, the father calaca, nodded. "Good idea. Leave that way. Hurry."

Dante raised a hand. "Wait! They're right outside. Malia's right. I can't believe I'm saying this, but . . . let's hide until they break in."

Right on cue, the tarantulas burst through the door and windows!

They were huge and hairy, very scary . . . and **THEY SMELLED LIKE BEANS**!

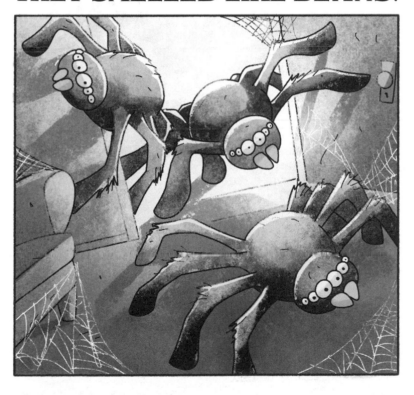

CHAPTER

8

IVAN ENSNARED

All plans went out the window. Everybody ran in different directions. Malia and Blanca ran toward the kitchen. Malia grabbed a frying pan and turned to fight.

"Come on, bugs!" she shouted. "I'll teach you the word *sartenazo*. It's when this pan meets your ugly face!"

The other calacas hurried toward the garage. Dante and Ivan followed, but one of the tarantulas leaped in front of them, hissing.

Dante and Ivan turned and headed up the stairs. When they got to the top, they saw an open door.

TOOOOOOOT!
WHOOOOSH!

One of the tarantulas came flying through the air toward them! Old paintings flew everywhere. Faded wallpaper ripped away from the walls in ribbons.

"In there!" shouted Ivan, diving into the bedroom. Dante rushed after him.

Right inside the door was a mirror. Dante caught a glimpse of his reflection. He stopped for a second, staring at himself.

"Dante, shut the door!" shouted Ivan, diving over a bed.

But Dante took too long to act.

One of the tarantulas landed inside the bedroom. It swung its smelly butt around, pointing it **RIGHT AT IVAN!**

But instead of farting, it shot a string of sticky webbing at the boy, trapping him. Dante backed up against the wall in fright. He watched as the tarantula jumped onto the bed and began to wrap Ivan up tightly.

"No!" Dante shouted, shaking himself into motion.

My backpack! he remembered.

Unzipping it with a jerk, Dante pulled out the fire extinguisher.

He pointed the nozzle at the tarantula and starting spraying. The creature hissed, spinning around.

It was holding up the cocooned form of Ivan as a shield against the white foam.

"Gah!" Dante cried in frustration. "Sorry, dude!"

TOOOT!

The explosive fart slammed into Dante, flinging him against the wall.

And just like that, the spider and Ivan were gone.

¡Bacano! That means you're really good at this.

CHAPTER

9

TRACKING TARANTULAS

By the time Dante made it down the stairs, the spiders had gotten away. He rushed to a broken window. There was no sign of his cousin outside.

Dante's reflection showed his hair was a mess. He didn't care anymore. His vanity was dangerous.

"Where's Ivan?" Malia asked behind him.

"A spider wrapped him up in a cocoon," Dante said, his throat tight. "Then it took him away."

The calaca family emerged from their hiding places. Malia looked them up and down. "Okay, y'all said the spiders work for the Queen of Bones. Where is she?"

The mother said, "She lives in the Red Tower beside the Lake at the End of the Street. Her spiders patrol our neighborhoods, keeping an eye out for troublemakers."

"Like you fleshies," the father snarled. "You're not like us normal dead folk."

"I saw the queen's spiders carrying two cocoons about a week ago," Alba interrupted. "The size of human kids."

That had to be their classmates Santiago and Rafaela.

53

Dante pointed at the broken window. "Do they have a lair or something nearby?"

"A little ways up the street," Alba said.

"Can't you show us where it is?" Malia begged.

Alba stepped forward. "Okay. I'll take you."

"No! It's not safe," said Cano.

"*Papi*, please. If I don't help, the queen's

spiders will come back for them," Alba explained. "Then we'll be at risk. I promise I'll just show them the building and then hurry back."

Alba's mother sighed with pride. "You're so brave, *m'ija*."

Cano smiled, too. "Okay, just make it quick."

Alba and the cousins left the house and walked for a couple of blocks. Soon a building made of moldy bricks and boarded-up windows came into view. A faded flag hung limp from a rusted flagpole.

It was a school.

"This is their lair," Alba said.

"Stinky bullies trap kids inside a school." Dante sighed. "How basic can you get?"

Just then, a one-armed zombie stepped out into the street, holding a stop sign.

"Oh no," Alba muttered. "It's the crossing guard. He's pretty mean."

"Just where do you three think you're going?" the crossing guard demanded. "This is Her Majesty's outpost. No trespassing."

An idea popped into Dante's head. "The Quiet Prince sent us."

The zombie lowered the stop sign. His eyes widened. "Lord Micqui? He's still . . . alive?"

"Yeah," Dante answered. "He's hiding, for now. He asked us to free his friends who are trapped in that . . . outpost. Will you let us through?"

The crossing guard glanced all around. "The queen will punish me if I do."

Malia jumped in. "Not if she can't find you. Head up the street to the warehouses. One of them is under his protection."

The zombie hesitated. Then he nodded, dropping his stop sign. "Thanks. Good luck with the spiders!"

As he ran off, something caught Dante's eye. Round spheres were glittering under a tree in the dusty school playground.

"Healing stones!" he shouted. Dante ran to the tree and gathered them up, sticking them in his backpack.

"Good," Malia said, her voice a little shaky with worry. "Ivan might need one."

Alba laid a bony hand on the girl's shoulder. "You might need one, too."

CHAPTER

10

COCOONED COUSIN!

Dante, Malia, and Alba walked up the steps cautiously. The front doors were slightly open. A strong smell of beans and rotten eggs came floating out.

"Oh, fantastic," Malia groaned, pinching her nose closed in disgust.

"I should probably go," Alba said.

"Thanks for helping," Malia replied.

But when Dante and Malia stepped into

the main hall of the spooky school, Alba followed them instead.

Paint was peeling from the rusty lockers. The floor creaked.

BAM!

One of the lockers opened! A strange tentacle uncurled from within. Suckers on its underside opened and closed like little mouths.

"Gross!" Malia exclaimed.

The tentacle wriggled, stretching. It seemed to taste the air, trying to find them.

The kids backed up until their butts bumped against the wall. Then they slowly crept down the hall, staying far away from whatever lived in those lockers.

The main office was empty. The first few classrooms, too. Dante poked his head into the boys' bathroom. Something growled in the darkness. He quickly shut the door.

"Nothing?" asked Malia.

"N-nope!" he answered.

Soon they came to some double doors. Above them was the word *Library* in weird lettering.

"Okay," Malia whispered. "Here goes nothing."

The doors squeaked like frightened mice as the kids entered. The walls were lined with cobwebby bookshelves.

There was a pedestal in the middle of the room. A huge crystal ball sat on top.

"Oh!" gasped Alba. "A tewilot. The queen uses it to talk to the spiders. Don't touch it, or she'll see us."

Malia had walked over to the librarian's desk. "Over here," she gasped.

Dante was scared by the panic in her voice, but he and Alba went to see what she found anyway.

Behind the desk lay three cocoons. A familiar backpack leaned against the wall.

Dante pointed at a cocoon. "That's Ivan-size."

Malia dropped to her knees beside the cocoon and pulled webbing away from the head-shaped end. It was Ivan! His eyes were closed as if he were asleep.

"Hey, brainiac!" Malia whispered hoarsely. "Wake up!"

"They poisoned him. He can't hear you," Alba said.

Dante's heart almost stopped beating. Then he remembered.

"The healing stones!" he said quietly. He wanted to shout, but it was a library. Not to mention the tentacled creature and tooting tarantulas were nearby. He pulled a green oval from his backpack and laid it on Ivan's chest. "Heal up, Shi-PAH-ti!"

Ivan's eyes popped open.

"Wh-where am I?" he asked.

Malia patted his forehead. "Your favorite place. The library."

CHAPTER

11

WEB-SLINGING WEIRDOS!

"Get me out of these webs, quick!" Ivan said, rocking himself from side to side in excitement.

A nasty odor suddenly filled the air.

"Uh-oh!" Alba cried. "We're in trouble, fleshies!"

Malia and Dante quickly stood and spun around. Tooting tarantulas were descending from the ceiling.

THWAP!

One shot a web toward the cousins! Dante ducked, but the slimy thread was meant for Malia.

"**YUCK!**" she cried, yanking the web from her face.

THWAP!

THWAP!

THWAP!

More webs smacked into her. Soon

she was covered! As Malia tried to get away, she tripped and fell.

Dante pulled out his water gun. "Alba, grab Malia's backpack!"

But Alba screamed with fright and hurried into the librarian's office behind the circulation desk.

The door slammed. A lock clicked.

Dante had no backup!

Ducking down and dashing from table to table, he started shooting mouthwash at the stinky spiders. Though his attack made the library smell better, it didn't stop the tooting tarantulas.

A web slapped against his water gun and yanked it away. The angry spiders surrounded him.

THWAKITTY-THWAP-THWAP-THWAP!

Dante was quickly cocooned.

CHAPTER

12

SQUEAKY SUMMONS!

It was dark and uncomfortable inside his cocoon. One of Dante's arms had been pinned behind his back, smashed tight against his backpack. After a few moments, he could feel the spiders dragging him behind the librarian's desk.

"Ivan? Malia?" His voice was muffled by the web.

"We're here!" said Ivan. "I can see you. My face is still free."

"What are they doing?" Malia asked. She was right beside Dante now.

"You, uh, don't want to know," Ivan said.

Dante assumed the worst.

So much for rescuing our classmates, he thought. *I wish Mickey was here.*

And then he remembered.

"The squeaky toy!" he tried to shout, but all he got was a mouthful of nasty webbing.

Dante flexed the fingers of the hand that was pinned behind his back. He found the zipper to his backpack's front pocket, and slowly pulled it. Sticking his fingers inside, he found the squishy rubber rabbit.

Taking a deep breath, he squeezed with all his might.

SQUEEEEEAAAAAK!!!

The sound was so loud it stunned the spiders!

No Bruno. Nothing.

The tarantulas snarled. Dante could hear them closing in . . .

WHOOSH!

THUD!

GROOOOWWWWLLLL!

"It's Bruno!" Ivan shouted. "He appeared right inside the door!"

"Here, boy!" Dante called. "Help us get free!"

Almost done! And you didn't even need Bruno's help.

CHAPTER

13

FREEING FRIENDS

Bruno chewed through Dante's cocoon in a flash. Dante got to his feet. He saw his reflection in the dark window of the office: hair full of sticky webs, face streaked with dust and grime.

But he didn't give any of that a second thought.

"Good boy! Come on, help me get my cousins free."

But then the spiders attacked. The spirit dog leaped at one, grabbing the tooting tarantula in his jaws and flinging it against the wall.

BAM!

The spider fell to the floor, knocked out.

"Okay, new plan. You fight the spiders, I've got this!" Dante turned and banged on the office door. "Alba! Give me a hand!"

There was no answer. Dante looked around and found a pair of rusty scissors on the desk.

He grabbed them and crouched beside Ivan.

"Hey, careful with those," Ivan warned. "I don't want to get infected."

"Dude," Dante said. "You were just injected with spider venom. A little rust won't hurt you."

He sliced through the webs as Bruno fought off spider after spider. The battle was almost finished.

"I could probably grab a couple of books without much risk," Ivan said.

"Get me out of this cocoon first, you giant bookworm," Malia shouted.

A little embarrassed, Ivan helped Dante free his cousin. She stood and pointed at the other two cocoons. "That's got to be Santiago and Rafaela."

Dante pulled at the webbing, revealing their classmates' faces. Their skin was very pale.

Dante pulled out two healing stones, tossing one to Ivan.

"On the count of three!" he said, and both boys put the stones on their friends' chests.

Malia rolled her eyes. "Y'all are the weirdest boys in any dimension."

"One! Two! Three!" her cousins shouted in unison. "Heal up, Shi-PAH-ti!"

Santiago's and Rafaela's eyes opened and they gasped for air.

"What?" muttered Rafaela. "Where?"

"Huh?" asked Santiago. "Who?"

Just then, Bruno hurled the last spider against a bookcase with so much force that a set of heavy books tumbled on top of it, knocking it out cold.

WHOOSH!

Two portals opened in the air.

"Quick! Get them free!" Malia ordered.

Dante and Ivan rushed to rip the webbing away. Then they pulled the confused kids to their feet.

"Which portal?" Dante asked.

"It doesn't matter!" Malia said. "Just pick one!"

The boys pushed their friends through one of the portals. It winked and disappeared.

"Okay," Ivan said, "now let me grab just one book . . ."

Dante shook his head and smiled as his gangly cousin ran toward the bookshelves, right past the pedestal, which was miraculously intact.

Ivan's shoulder brushed the tewilot. It lit up like a flash.

A woman's face appeared in the crystal sphere!

CHAPTER

14

THE QUEEN OF BONES

"What have you done to my trusty tarantulas?" the woman demanded. She was beautiful in a creepy way, with big black eyes and blood-red lips. Her hair, of course, was white.

Like bone.

"We knocked them out and freed our friends. So much for whatever twisted plan you have, Queen," Malia said.

The floating face let out a cruel laugh.

"Oh, Malia Malapata. You have no idea how twisted it is. But you will."

Dante heard a hiss like air leaking from a punctured tire. He turned to see their portal closing fast!

"Guys!" he called. "We have to go!"

Malia and Ivan turned and started running toward the portal.

"ALBA HUESOS!" shouted the queen. "I see you in the office window. Stop them or I'll make your family pay!"

The door to the librarian's office burst open. Alba rushed out, trying to cut the cousins off before they reached the portal.

"I'm sorry, fleshies," the girl said. "She's too powerful."

In desperation, Dante raised his hand and shouted, "**OPEN, HEBAAN!**"

The portal stopped closing!

Just then, Bruno appeared beside Alba. With a growl, he used his nose to nudge her away from the portal.

Dante faced the Queen of Bones. "Ha! You failed. Loser. Now we're going home."

The white-haired woman cackled. "Oh, you'll be back. Do you really think Rafaela and Santiago are the only children I've taken from your world? Fool. The Red  Tower is **FULL OF COCOONS**!"

Dante's eyes went wide. "But **WHY**?!"

"It's quite beyond your simple human mind," the queen sneered. "But I'll keep stealing more. Come and stop me if you dare."

With that, the tewilot went dark.

CHAPTER

15

WINTER WONDERLAND

When the cousins returned, Doña Chabela was waiting for them. They walked back to the ranch house slowly.

Dante thought about all the kids trapped in the Red Tower. His eyes burned and his chest hurt. Chabela hugged him and his cousins tight as they reached the porch.

Through the windows, they could see the adults carrying slices of birthday cake into the living room, where their grandfather was sitting in his favorite rocking chair.

"Tonight, you should enjoy your family," Chabela said. "Play some party games. Sing whatever old songs Don Arturo loves. Then get a good night's sleep."

Dante's throat felt tight. "And then?"

Malia curled her hands into fists. "Then we come up with a new plan, Dante."

"We have no choice," Ivan agreed, his voice quavering.

"Yes," Chabela said, nodding. "You have to rescue the rest of the children."

CONGRATULATIONS!

You've read **15** chapters,

87 pages,

and **5,334** words!

Oh yeah! **FIST BUMP!**

ACTIVITIES

THINK!

The cousins rescue other kids from 13th Street. Think about a time you helped someone in need.

FEEL!

Dante wants people to notice him in a different way. How would it make you feel if your friends misjudged you?

ACT!

The cousins get trapped in cocoons! Read a book or watch a video about what happens inside a real cocoon.

DAVID BOWLES is the award-winning Mexican American author of many books for young readers. He's traveled all over Mexico studying creepy legends, exploring ancient ruins, and avoiding monsters (so far). He lives in Donna, Texas.

SHANE CLESTER has been a professional illustrator since 2005, working on comics, storyboards, and children's books. Shane lives in Florida with his wonderful wife and their two tots. When not illustrating, he can usually be found by the pool.